The Pout-Pout Fish
Far, Far from Home

Deborah Diesen

Pictures by **Dan Hanna**

Farrar Straus Giroux • New York

*For my friend April, with love across the
miles and through the years* —D.D.

*For all my traveling companions from
throughout the years* —D.H.

Farrar Straus Giroux Books for Young Readers
An imprint of Macmillan Publishing Group, LLC
175 Fifth Avenue, New York 10010

Text copyright © 2017 by Deborah Diesen
Pictures copyright © 2017 by Dan Hanna
All rights reserved
Color separations by Embassy Graphics
Printed in China by RR Donnelley Asia Printing Solutions, Ltd.,
Dongguan City, Guangdong Province
Designed by Roberta Pressel
First edition, 2017
10 9 8 7 6 5 4 3 2 1

mackids.com

Library of Congress Cataloging-in-Publication Data
Names: Diesen, Deborah, author. | Hanna, Dan, illustrator.
Title: The pout-pout fish, far, far from home / Deborah Diesen ; pictures by
    Dan Hanna.
Description: First edition. | New York : Farrar Straus Giroux, 2017. |
    Series: A Pout-pout fish adventure | Summary: "Mr. Fish is going on vacation,
    but what happens when he forgets his favorite toy?"— Provided by publisher.
Identifiers: LCCN 2016001911 | ISBN 9780374301941 (hardback)
Subjects: | CYAC: Stories in rhyme. | Fishes—Fiction. | Travel—Fiction. |
    Vacations—Fiction. | Self-reliance—Fiction. | BISAC: JUVENILE FICTION /
    Animals / Fishes. | JUVENILE FICTION / Social Issues / Emotions & Feelings.
Classification: LCC PZ8.3.D565 Pop 2017 | DDC [E]—dc23
LC record available at https://lccn.loc.gov/2016001911

Our books may be purchased in bulk for promotional, educational, or business use. Please
contact your local bookseller or the Macmillan Corporate and Premium Sales Department
at (800) 221-7945 ext. 5442 or by e-mail at MacmillanSpecialMarkets@macmillan.com.

Mr. Fish sent off for flyers
And he studied each location,
Then he picked the perfect place
For his *very first vacation*!

"Amazing sights to see,
And only one day's journey there!"
So he planned and he prepped
And he packed his bags with care.

"I'm a fish who'd like to travel.
I'm a fish who'd like to roam.
And I'm ready for adventure
On my trip away from home!"

He started bright and early,
Feeling fresh and fishy-fine,
And his trip was going great . . .

. . . till a flashing orange sign!

"May I help?" asked a ray.
"Do you need a local map?
There's an easy way around it—
You can be there in a snap!"

Mr. Fish said, "Thanks!"
And he started off anew.
The route he maneuvered
Had a *marvelous* view!

"I'm a fish who loves to travel.
I'm a fish who loves to roam.
And I'm having an adventure
On my trip away from home!"

He circled 'round the roundabout
And soon was back on track,
And his trip was going great . . .

. . . till he reached for his snack!

"May I help?" asked an eel.
"Do you need a place to eat?
There's a briny-good diner
On the very next street."

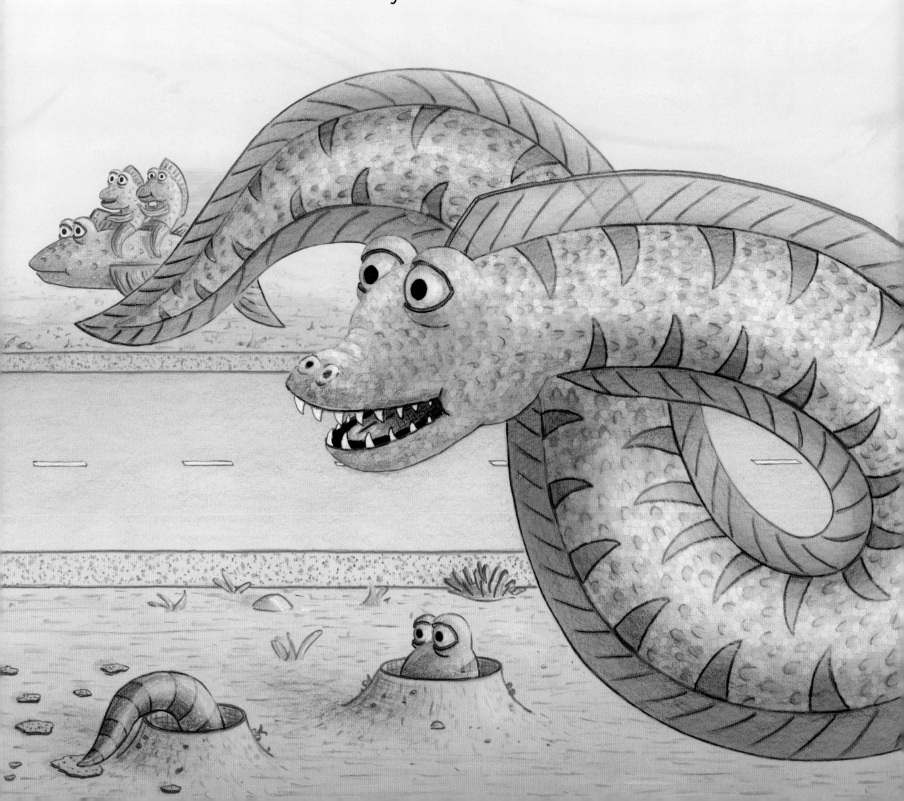

Mr. Fish said, "Thanks!"
And he quickly found the place.
Their flavorful creations
Put a *smile* on his face!

"I'm a fish who loves to travel.
I'm a fish who loves to roam.
And I'm having an adventure
On my trip away from home!"

. . . till a *bump* jarred his load.

"May I help?" asked a crab.
"Seems your luggage overflowed!
There's a rest stop ahead—
We can re-secure your load."

Mr. Fish said, "Thanks!"
And they handled the repair.
His day had been exhausting,
But the end was nearly there!

"I'm a fish who loves to travel.
I'm a fish who loves to roam.
And I'm having an adventure
On my trip away from home!"

He finally reached the lodge,
Found his room, and got unpacked.
And his trip was going great . . .

. . . till he saw what he lacked!

"Oh, I really thought I brought it!"
And his heart beat faster.
"I forgot my snoozy-snuggly!
My vacation's a disaster!

"I *don't* like to travel
And I *don't* like to roam.
This is *not* a great adventure—
I just want to go *home*!"

He felt sad and dreary-weary.
All his plans were falling through.
But he'd come *so* far—
Was there *something* he could do?

He took a *deeeep* breath.
It soothed his commotion.
A thought reached out
All the way across the ocean:

Feeling warm and snug with love,
Mr. Fish fell asleep,

And he woke the next morning
With exciting plans to keep!

His vacation was *fin-tastic*,
Full of happy and hurrah.

What amusing things he tried!
What amazing sights he saw!

When his trip was finally over,
He reflected on his stay:

The things that he had learned
And who he'd met along the way.

"Not every single part
Of a trip goes swell,
But the detours and the bumps
Are the trip as well.

"I'm a fish who loves to travel!
I'm a fish who loves to roam!
And I had a great adventure . . .

... Now it's nice to be back home!"